STACKS OF TROUBLE

by Martha F. Brenner
Illustrated by Liza Woodruff

The Kane Press
New York

Book Design/Art Direction: Roberta Pressel

Library of Congress Cataloging-in-Publication Data

Brenner, Martha.
    Stacks of trouble/Martha F. Brenner; illustrated by Liza Woodruff.
      p. cm. — (Math matters.)
    Summary: Mike learns how fast dirty dishes can pile up when he tries to avoid washing them.
    ISBN 1-57565-098-3 (pbk. : alk. paper)
    [1. Dishwashing—Fiction.] I. Woodruff, Liza, ill. II. Title. III. Series.
    PZ7.B75183 St 2000
    [Fic]—dc21
                                             99-088839
                                            CIP
                                           AC

10 9 8 7 6 5 4 3 2 1

First published in the United States of America in 2000 by The Kane Press.
Printed in Hong Kong.

MATH MATTERS is a registered trademark of The Kane Press.

My mother likes our house clean at all times. Don't ask me why. We hoped we'd get a break when she went to help Aunt Sue with the new baby. No chance.

She left a long list of jobs.

I picked an easy job—washing the dishes.
You just load the dishwasher, push a button,
and swish! The machine does it all.

I decided to feed Wolfie, too—that's not
work. There's nothing I hate more than work.

Was I in for a surprise. After breakfast I went to open the dishwasher. That's when I saw the note. Oh, no! I'd have to wash dishes by hand. It would take forever!

Besides, I had important things to do. Wolfie and I had to practice. The Frisbee contest was only one day away!

"Calm down," I told myself. There weren't many dirty dishes. I didn't need to wash them yet.

We had lots of clean dishes, enough to last until the dishwasher was fixed. The repairman was coming the next day.

Then at lunch time my brother John made messy tuna sandwiches. "We don't need plates for sandwiches!" I said. "Let's use paper towels."

"I don't want to eat off a towel," my sister Lisa said. She wrinkled her nose.

Oh, well. We didn't use a lot of dishes.
In fact, it wouldn't take long to wash them…

Just then my friend Sal knocked on the
back door. The Crunch brothers had dared
us in touch football. "We won't have a
chance unless you play," said Sal.

I decided the dirty dishes could wait.

We weren't as tall as the Crunchs or as fast. But they always ran the same plays. *Duh!* So I figured out how to block them. My passes flew like bullets. We won!

We celebrated at my house. Popcorn and potato chips. No dishes needed! Then someone had a glass of juice. So everyone had juice—except me.

Lisa and her friends were giving each other makeovers. They came in for ice cream. So everyone had ice cream— except me. Was this any way to thank a football hero? With dirty dishes?

Dad wasn't going to like the mess. I was afraid he'd make me start washing. So I cleaned up—a little. I stacked the dishes. Then I hid a few in the basement.

5 dishes
x 2 stacks
10 dirty dishes

I couldn't put this job off much longer. But I could stop people from dirtying EXTRA dishes. I taped up a warning on the kitchen door.

Lisa invited her friends to stay overnight.
The girls—excuse me, the supermodels—
showed off their new looks at dinner.

I didn't pay much attention. I was
too busy looking at the dishes. There
were eighteen, not counting
the serving bowls!

More people meant more dirty dishes. Lots more. The kitchen was starting to smell funny.

Time for another trip to the basement.

I dragged myself up and down those basement stairs. What I needed was a good night's sleep. It was a lot of work not doing the dishes.

I overslept! If I didn't hurry, we'd miss the Frisbee contest. Everybody else had already had breakfast. I took the last clean bowl.

The kitchen smelled like dirty socks and rotten eggs. "That repairman better hurry," I told myself.

I aimed the Frisbee high. Wolfie caught
it with all paws off the ground. The judges
gave him extra points. What a dog! What a
thrower! We won second prize.

When we got home, it was almost time to set the table for lunch. I looked in the cupboards. No clean plates. Only two glasses. I looked in the silverware drawer. Empty.

≈ MEMO ≈
DISHWASHER
BROKEN

DO NOT USE
REPAIRMAN
COMING
TOMORROW
—Mom

But it was stupid to wash dishes BEFORE lunch. I bet I could find something else to use. What's a dish, anyway? Just a food holder!

I found some things that were just as good as regular dishes. Better really. Much more interesting.

"Mike! You dish brain," John said.

"What *were* you thinking?" Lisa giggled.

They just didn't get it. I started to wonder how Dad would take it. I soon found out....

Boy, was I in trouble. Guess what Dad
found in the basement? *Aargh!* Dad said
I'd gone too far. My family was counting
on me to do my job.

I carried the dishes up fast. What *had* I been thinking?

I bet there were more dirty dishes here than anyone anywhere had ever washed. Could I set a record?

I took a deep breath and plunged in.
I soaked. I scrubbed. I rinsed. Soon the
clean dishes equaled the dirty ones. I
began to feel better. But there was
more work to do.

Just as I was washing the last few dishes, who should walk in? The repairman! Some luck. He shook his head when he saw what I was doing.

"Dirty dishes sure can multiply," he said.
No kidding!

MULTIPLICATION CHART

Here are some ways to multiply.

1. Use models.

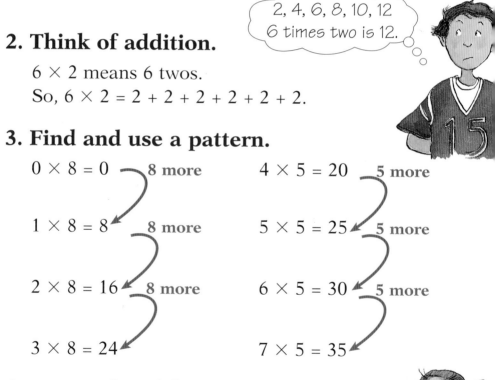

2 equal groups of 4 pans
2 × 4 = 8 pans

3 equal groups of 5 spoons
3 × 5 =15 spoons

2, 4, 6, 8, 10, 12
6 times two is 12.

2. Think of addition.

6 × 2 means 6 twos.
So, 6 × 2 = 2 + 2 + 2 + 2 + 2 + 2.

3. Find and use a pattern.

0 × 8 = 0 ⟶ **8 more**

1 × 8 = 8 **8 more**

2 × 8 = 16 **8 more**

3 × 8 = 24

4 × 5 = 20 **5 more**

5 × 5 = 25 **5 more**

6 × 5 = 30 **5 more**

7 × 5 = 35

4. Use a related fact.

9 × 3 = ?

I know 3 × 9 = 27.
So, 9 × 3 = 27.